MOON OF ZAMBEBWEI

BY

ROBERT E. HOWARD

British Library Cataloguing-in-Publication Data
A catalogue record for this book is available from the
British Library

Contents

Robert E. Howard

Robert Ervin Howard was born in Peaster, Texas in 1906. During his youth, his family moved between a variety of Texan boomtowns, and Howard – a bookish and somewhat introverted child – was steeped in the violent myths and legends of the Old South. Although he loved reading and learning, Howard developed a distinctly Texan, hardboiled outlook on the world. He became a passionate fan of boxing, taking it up at an amateur level, and from the age of nine began to write adventure tales of semi-historical bloodshed. In 1919, when Howard was thirteen, his family moved to the Central Texas hamlet of Cross Plains, where he would stay for the rest of his life.

At fifteen Howard began to read the pulp magazines of the day, and to write more seriously. The December 1922 issue of his high school newspaper featured two of his stories, 'Golden Hope Christmas' and 'West is West'. In 1924 he sold his first piece – a short caveman tale titled 'Spear and Fang' – for $16 to the not-yet-famous *Weird Tales* magazine. He published with the magazine regularly over the next few years. 1929 was a breakout year for Howard, in that the 23-year-old writer began to sell to other magazines, such as *Ghost Stories* and *Argosy*, both of whom had previously sent him hundreds of rejection slips. In 1930, he began a

1

correspondence with weird fiction master H. P. Lovecraft which ran up to his death six years later, and is regarded as one of the great correspondence cycles in all of fantasy literature.

It was partly due to Lovecraft's encouragement that Howard created his most famous character, Conan the Cimmerian. Conan – a barbarian-turned-King during the Hyborian Age, a mythical period of some 12,000 years ago – featured in seventeen *Weird Tales* stories between 1933 and 1936, and is now regarded as having spawned the 'sword and sorcery' genre, making Howard's influence on fantasy literature comparable to that of J. R. R. Tolkien's. The Conan stories have since been adapted many times, most famously in the series of films starring Arnold Schwarzenegger.

Howard was enjoying an all-time high in sales by the beginning of 1936, but he was also deeply upset by the ill health of his mother, who had fallen into a coma. On the morning of June 11, 1936, he asked an attending nurse whether she would ever recover, and the nurse replied negatively. Howard walked to his car, parked outside the family home in Cross Plains, and shot himself. He died eight hours later, aged just thirty.

CHAPTER 1.
THE HORROR IN THE PINES

The silence of the pine woods lay like a brooding cloak about the soul of Bristol McGrath. The black shadows seemed fixed, immovable as the weight of superstition that overhung this forgotten back-country. Vague ancestral dreads stirred at the back of McGrath's mind; for he was born in the pine woods, and sixteen years of roaming about the world had not erased their shadows. The fearsome tales at which he had shuddered as a child whispered again in his consciousness; tales of black shapes stalking the midnight glades . . . .

Cursing these childish memories, McGrath quickened his pace. The dim trail wound tortuously between dense walls of giant trees. No wonder he had been unable to hire anyone in the distant river village to drive him to the Ballville estate. The road was impassable for a vehicle, choked with rotting stumps and new growth. Ahead of him it bent sharply.

McGrath halted short, frozen to immobility. The silence had been broken at last, in such a way as to bring a chill tingling to the backs of his hands. For the sound had been the unmistakable groan of a human being in agony. Only for an instant was McGrath motionless. Then he was gliding about the bend of the trail with the noiseless slouch of a hunting panther.

A blue snub-nosed revolver had appeared as if by magic in his right hand. His left involuntarily clenched in his pocket on the bit of paper that was responsible for his presence in that grim forest. That paper was a frantic and mysterious appeal for aid; it was signed by McGrath's worst enemy, and contained the name of a woman long dead.

McGrath rounded the bend in the trail, every nerve tense and alert, expecting anything--except what he actually saw. His startled eyes hung on the grisly object for an instant, and then swept the forest walls. Nothing stirred there. A dozen feet back from the trail visibility vanished in a ghoulish twilight, where anything might lurk unseen. McGrath dropped to his knee beside the figure that lay in the trail before him.

It was a man, spread-eagled, hands and feet bound to four pegs driven deeply in the hard-packed earth; a blackbearded, hook-nosed, swarthy man. "Ahmed!", muttered McGrath. "Ballville's Arab Servant! God!"

For it was not the binding cords that brought the glaze to the Arab's eyes. A weaker man than McGrath might have sickened at the mutilations which keen knives had wrought on the man's body. McGrath recognized the work of an expert in the art of torture. Yet a spark of life still throbbed in the tough frame of the Arab. McGrath's gray eyes grew bleaker as he noted the position of the victim's body, and his-mind flew back to another, grimmer jungle, and a halfflayed black man pegged out on a path as a warning to the white man who dared invade a forbidden land.

He cut the cords, shifted the dying man to a more comfortable position. It was all he could do. He saw the delirium ebb momentarily in the bloodshot eyes, saw recognition glimmer there. Clots of bloody foam splashed the matted beard. The lips writhed soundlessly, and McGrath glimpsed the bloody stump of a severed tongue.

The black-nailed fingers began scrabbling in the dust. They shook, clawing erratically, but with purpose. McGrath bent close, tense with interest, and saw crooked lines grow under the quivering fingers. With the last effort of an iron will, the Arab was tracing a message in the characters of his own language. McGrath recognized the name: "Richard Ballville"; it was followed by "danger," and the hand waved weakly up the trail; then--and McGrath stiffened convulsively--"Constance." One final effort of the dragging finger traced "John De Al--".

Suddenly the bloody frame was convulsed by one last sharp agony; the lean, sinewy hand knotted spasmodically and then fell limp. Ahmed ibn Suleyman was beyond vengeance or mercy.

McGrath rose, dusting his hands, aware of the tense stillness of the grim woods around him; aware of a faint rustling in their depths that was not caused by any breeze. He looked down at the mangled figure with involuntary

pity, though he knew well the foulness of the Arab's heart, a
black evil that had matched that of Ahmed's master, Richard
Ballville. Well, it seemed that master and man had at last met
their match in human fiendishness. But who, or what? For
a hundred years the Ballvilles had ruled supreme over this
back-country, first over their wide plantations and hundreds
of slaves, and later over the submissive descendants of those
slaves. Richard, the last of the Ballvilles, had exercised as
much authority over the pinelands as any of his autocratic
ancestors. Yet from this country where men had bowed to
the Ballvilles for a century, had come that frenzied cry of
fear, a telegram that McGrath clenched in his coat pocket.

Stillness succeeded the rustling, more sinister than any
sound. McGrath knew he was watched; knew that the spot
where Ahmed's body lay was the iovisible deadline that had
been drawn for him. He believed that he would be allowed to
turn and retrace his steps unmolested to the distant village.
He knew that if he continued on his way, death would strike
him suddenly and unseen. Turning, he strode back the way
he had come.

He made the turn and kept straight on until he had
passed another crook in the trail. Then he halted, listened.
All was silent. Quickly he drew the paper from his pocket,
smoothed out the wrinkles and read, again, in the cramped
scrawl of the man he hated most on earth:

Bristol:

If you still love Constance Brand, for God's sake forget your hate and come to Ballville Manor as quickly as the devil can drive you.

RICHARD BALLVILLE.

That was all. It reached him by telegraph in that Far Western city where McGrath had resided since his return from Africa. He would have ignored it, but for the mention of Constance Brand. That name had sent a choking, agonizing pulse of amazement through his soul, had sent him racing toward the land of his birth by train and plane, as if, indeed, the devil were on his heels. It was the name of one he thought dead for three years; the name of the only woman Bristol McGrath had ever loved.

Replacing the telegram, he left the trail and headed westward, pushing his powerful frame between the thickset trees. His feet made little sound on the matted pine needles. His progress was all but noiseless. Not for nothing had he spent his boyhood in the country of the big pines.

Three hundred yards from the old road he came upon that which he sought-an ancient trail paralleling the road. Choked with young growth, it was little more than a trace through the thick pines. He knew that it ran to the back of the Ballville mansion; did not believe the secret watchers would be guarding it. For how could they know he remembered it?

He hurried south along it, his ears whetted for any sound. Sight alone could not be trusted in that forest. The mansion, he knew, was not far away, now. He was passing through what had once been fields, in the days of Richard's grandfather, running almost up to the spacious lawns that girdled the Manor. But for half a century they had been abandoned to the advance of the forest.

But now he glimpsed the Manor, a hint of solid bulk among the pine tops ahead of him. And almost simultaneously his heart shot into his throat as a scream of human anguish knifed the stillness. He could not tell whether it was a man or a woman who screamed, and his thought that it might be a woman winged his feet in his reckless dash toward the building that loomed starkly up just beyond the straggling fringe of trees.

The young pines had even invaded the once generous lawns. The whole place wore an aspect of decay. Behind the Manor, the barns, and outhouses which once housed slave families, were crumbling in ruin. The mansion itself seemed to totter above the litter, a creaky giant, ratgnawed and rotting, ready to collapse at any untoward event. With the stealthy tread of a tiger Bristol McGrath approached a window on the side of the house. From that window sounds were issuing that were an affront to the tree-filtered sunlight and a crawling horror to the brain.

Nerving himself for what he might see, he peered within.

CHAPTER 2.
BLACK TORTURE

He was looking into a great dusty chamber which might have served as a ballroom in ante-bellum days; its lofty ceiling was hung with cobwebs, its rich oak panels showed dark and stained. But there was a fire in the great fireplace-a small fire, just large enough to heat to a white glow the slender steel rods thrust into it.

But it was only later that Bristol McGrath saw the fire and the things that glowed on the hearth. His eyes were gripped like a spell on the master of the Manor; and once again he looked on a dying man.

A heavy beam had been nailed to the paneled wall, and from it jutted a rude cross-piece. From this cross-piece Richard Ballville hung by cords about his wrists. His toes barely touched the floor, tantalizingly, inviting him to stretch his frame continually in an effort to relieve the agonizing strain on his arms. The cords had cut deeply into his wrists; blood trickled down his arms; his hands were black and swollen almost to bursting. He was naked except for his trousers, and McGrath saw that already the white-hot irons had been horribly employed. There was reason enough for the deathly pallor of the man, the cold beads of agony upon his skin. Only his fierce vitality had allowed him thus long to survive the ghastly burns on his limbs and body.

On his breast had been burned a curious symbol-a cold hand laid itself on McGrath's spine. For he recognized that symbol, and once again his memory raced away across the world and the years to a black, grim, hideous jungle where drums bellowed in fire-shot darkness and naked priests of an abhorred cult traced a frightful symbol in quivering human flesh.

Between the fireplace and the dying man squatted a thick-set black man, clad only in ragged, muddy trousers.

His back was toward the window, presenting an impressive pair of shoulders. His bullet-head was set squarely between those gigantic shoulders, like that of a frog, and he appeared to be avidly watching the face of the man on the cross-piece.

Richard Ballville's bloodshot eyes were like those of a tortured animal, but they were fully sane and conscious: they blazed with desperate vitality. He lifted his head painfully and his gaze swept the room. Outside the window McGrath instinctively shrank back. He did not know whether Ballville saw him or not. The man showed no sign to betray the presence of the watcher to the bestial black who scrutinized him. Then the brute turned his head toward the fire, reaching a long ape-like arm toward a glowing iron-and Ballville's eyes blazed with a fierce and urgent meaning

11

the watcher could not mistake. McGrath did not need the agonized motion of the tortured head that accompanied the look. With a tigerish bound he was over the window-sill and in the room, even as the startled black shot erect, whirling with apish agility.

McGrath had not drawn his gun. He dared not risk a shot that might bring other foes upon him. There was a butcher-knife in the belt that held up the ragged, muddy trousers. It seemed to leap like a living thing into the hand of the black as he turned. But in McGrath's hand gleamed a curved Afghan dagger that had served him well in many a bygone battle.

Knowing the advantage of instant and relentless attack, he did not pause. His feet scarcely touched the floor inside before they were hurling him at the astounded black man.

An inarticulate cry burst from the thick red lips. The eyes rolled wildly, the butcher-knife went back and hissed forward with the swiftness of a striking cobra that would have disembowled a man whose thews were less steely than those of Bristol McGrath.

But the black was involuntarily stumbling backward as he struck, and that instinctive action slowed his stroke just enough for McGrath to avoid it with a lightning-like twist of his torso. The long blade hissed under his arm-pit, slicing cloth and skin-and simultaneously the Afghan dagger ripped through the black, bull throat.

There was no cry, but only a choking gurgle as the man fell, spouting blood. McGrath had sprung free as a wolf springs after delivering the death-stroke. Without emotion he surveyed his handiwork. The black man was already dead, his head half severed from his body. That slicing sidewise lunge that slew in silence, severing the throat to the spinal column, was a favorite stroke of the hairy hillmen that haunt the crags overhanging the Khyber Pass. Less than a dozen white men have ever mastered it. Bristol McGrath was one.

McGrath turned to Richard Ballville. Foam dripped on the seared, naked breast, and blood trickled from the lips. McGrath feared that Ballville had suffered the same mutilation that had rendered Ahmed speechless; but it was only suffering and shock that numbed Ballville's tongue. McGrath cut his cords and eased him down on a worn old divan near by. Ballville's lean, muscle-corded body quivered like taut steel strings under McGrath's hands. He gagged, finding his voice.

"I knew you'd come!" he gasped, writhing at the contact of the divan against his seared flesh. "I've hated you for years, but I knew-"

McGrath's voice was harsh as the rasp of steel. "What did you mean by your mention of Constance Brand? She is dead."

A ghastly smile twisted the thin lips.

"No, she's not dead! But she soon will be, if you don't hurry. Quick! Brandy! There on the table-that beast didn't drink it all."

McGrath held the bottle to his lips; Ballville drank avidly. McGrath wondered at the man's iron nerve. That he was in ghastly agony was obvious. He should be screaming in a delirium of pain. Yet he held to sanity and spoke lucidly, though his voice was a laboring croak.

"I haven't much time," he choked. "Don't interrupt. Save your curses till later. We both loved Constance Brand. She loved you. Three years ago she disappeared. Her garments were found on the bank of a river. Her body was never recovered. You went to Africa to drown your sorrow; I retired to the estate of my ancestors and became a recluse.

"What you didn't know-what the world didn't know- -was that Constance Brand came with me! No, she didn't drown. That ruse was my idea. For three years Constance Brand has lived in this house!" He achieved a ghastly laugh. "Oh, don't look so stunned, Bristol. She didn't come of her own free will. She loved you too much. I kidnapped her, brought her here by force-Bristol!" His voice rose to a frantic shriek. "If you kill me you'll never learn where she is!"

The frenzied hands that had locked on his corded throat relaxed and sanity returned to the red eyes of Bristol McGrath.

"Go on," he whispered in a voice not even he recognized.

"I couldn't help it," gasped the dying man. "She was the only woman I ever loved-oh, don't sneer, Bristol. The others didn't count. I brought her here where I was king. She couldn't escape, couldn't get word to the outside world. No one lives in this section except nigger descendants of the slaves owned by my family. My word is-was-their only law.

"I swear I didn't harm her. I only kept her prisoner, trying to force her to marry me. I didn't want her any other way. I was mad, but I couldn't help it. I come of a race of autocrats who took what they wanted, recognized no law but their own desires. You know that. You understand it. You come of the same breed yourself.

"Constance hates me, if that's any consolation to you, damn you. She's strong, too. I thought I could break her spirit. But I couldn't, not without the whip, and I couldn't bear to use that." He grinned hideously at the wild growl that rose unbidden to McGrath's lips. The big man's eyes were coals of fire; his hard hands knotted into iron mallets.

A spasm racked Ballville, and blood started from his lips. His grin faded and he hurried on.

"All went well until the foul fiend inspired me to send for John De Albor. I met him in Vienna, years ago. He's from East Africa-a devil in human form! He saw Constance-lusted for her as only a man of his type can. When I finally

15

realized that, I tried to kill him. Then I found that he was stronger than I; that he'd made himself master of the niggers-my niggers, to whom my word had always been law. He told them his devilish cult-'

"Voodoo," muttered McGrath involuntarily.

"No! Voodoo is infantile beside this black fiendishness. Look at the symbol on my breast, where De Albor burned it with a white-hot iron. You have been in Africa. You understand the brand of Zambebwei.

"De Albor turned my negroes against me. I tried to escape with Constance and Ahmed. My own blacks hemmed me in. I did smuggle a telegram through to the village by a man who remained faithful to me--they suspected him and tortured him until he admitted it. John De Albor brought me his head.

"Before the final break I hid Constance in a place where no one will ever find her, except you. De Albor tortured Ahmed until he told that I had sent for a friend of the girl's to aid us. Then De Albor sent his men up the road with what was left of Ahmed, as a warning to you if you came. It was this morning that they seized us; I hid Constance last night. Not even Ahmed knew where. De Albor tortured me to make me tell-" the dying man's hands clenched and a fierce passionate light blazed in his eyes. McGrath knew that not all the torments of all the hells could ever have wrung that secret from Ballville's iron lips.

16

"It was the least you could do," he said, his voice harsh with conflicting emotions. "I've lived in hell for three years because of you-and Constance has. You deserve to die. If you weren't dying already I'd kill you myself."

"Damn you, do you think I want your forgiveness?" gasped the dying man. "I'm glad you suffered. If Constance didn't need your help, I'd like to see you dying as I'm dying-and I'll be waiting for you in hell. But enough of this. De Albor left me awhile to go up the road and assure himself that Ahmed was dead. This beast got to swilling my brandy and decided to torture me some himself.

"Now listen-Constance is hidden in Lost Cave. No man on earth knows of its existence except you and menot even the negroes. Long ago I put an iron door in the entrance, and I killed the man who did the work; so the secret is safe. There's no key. You've got to open it by working certain knobs."

It was more and more difficult for the man to enunciate intelligibly. Sweat dripped from his face, and the cords of his arms quivered.

"Run your fingers over the edge of the door until you find three knobs that form a triangle. You can't see them; you'll have to feel. Press each one in counter-clockwise motion, three times, around and around. Then pull on the bar. The door will open. Take Constance and fight your way out. If you see they're going to get you, shoot her! Don't let her fall into the hands of that black beast-"

The voice rose to a shriek, foam spattered from the livid writhing lips, and Richard Ballville heaved himself almost upright, then toppled limply back. The iron will that had animated the broken body had snapped at last, as a taut wire snaps.

McGrath looked down at the still form, his brain a maelstrom of seething emotions, then wheeled, glaring, every nerve atingle, his pistol springing into his hand.

CHAPTER 3.
THE BLACK PRIEST

A man stood in the doorway that opened upon the great outer hall-a tall man in a strange alien garb. He wore a turban and a silk coat belted with a gay-hued girdle. Turkish slippers were on his feet. His skin was not much darker than McGrath's, his features distinctly oriental in spite of the heavy glasses he wore.

"Who the devil are you?" demanded McGrath, covering him.

"Ali ibn Suleyman, effendi," answered the other in faultless Arabic. "I came to this place of devils at the urging of my brother, Ahmed ibn Suleyman, whose soul may the Prophet ease. In New Orleans the letter came to me. I hastened here. And lo, stealing through the woods, I saw black men dragging my brother's corpse to the river. I came on, seeking his master."

McGrath mutely indicated the dead man. The Arab bowed his head in stately reverence.

"My brother loved him," he said. "I would have vengeance for my brother and my brother's master. Ef fendi, let me go with you."

"All right." McGrath was afire with impatience. He knew the fanatical clan-loyalty of the Arabs, knew that

Ahmed's one decent trait had been a fierce devotion for the scoundrel he served. "Follow me."

With a last glance at the master of the Manor and the black body sprawling like a human sacrifice before him, McGrath left the chamber of torture. Just so, he reflected,' one of Ballville's warrior-king ancestors might have lain in some dim past age, with a slaughtered slave at his feet to serve his spirit in the land of ghosts.

With the Arab at his heels, McGrath emerged into the girdling pines that slumbered in the still heat of the noon. Faintly to his ears a distant pulse of sound was borne by a vagrant drift of breeze. It sounded like the throb of a faraway drum.

"Come on!" McGrath strode through the cluster of outhouses and plunged into the woods that rose behind them. Here, too, had once stretched the fields that builded the wealth of the aristocratic Ballvilles; but for many years they had been abandoned. Paths straggled aimlessly through the ragged growth, until presently the growing denseness of the trees told the invaders that they were in forest that had never known the woodsman's ax. McGrath looked for a path. Impressions received in childhood are always enduring. Memory remains, overlaid by later things, but unerring through the years. McGrath found the path he sought, a dim trace, twisting through the trees.

They were forced to walk single file; the branches scraped their clothing, their feet sank into the carpet of pine needles. The land trended gradually lower. Pines gave way to cypresses, choked with underbrush. Scummy pools of stagnant water glimmered under the trees. Bullfrogs croaked, mosquitoes sang with maddening insistence about them. Again the distant drum throbbed across the pinelands.

McGrath shook the sweat out of his eyes. That drum roused memories well fitted to these somber surroundings. His thoughts reverted to the hideous scar seared on Richard Ballville's naked breast. Ballville had supposed that he, McGrath, knew its meaning; but he did not. That it portended black horror and madness he knew, but its full significance he did not know. Only once before had he seen that symbol, in the horror-haunted country of Zambebwei, into which few white men had ever ventured, and from which only one white man had ever escaped alive. Bristol McGrath was that man, and he had only penetrated the fringe of that abysmal land of jungle and black swamp. He had not been able to plunge deep enough into that forbidden realm either to prove or to disprove the ghastly tales men whispered of an ancient cult surviving a prehistoric age, of the worship of a monstrosity whose mold violated an accepted law of nature. Little enough he had seen; but what he had seen had filled him with shuddering horror that sometimes returned now in crimson nightmares.

No word had passed between the men since they had left the Manor. McGrath plunged on through the vegetation that choked the path. A fat, blunt-tailed moccasin slithered from under his feet and vanished. Water could not be far away; a few more steps revealed it. They stood on the edge of a dank, slimy marsh from which rose a miasma of rotting vegetable matter. Cypresses shadowed it. The path ended at its edge. The swamp stretched away and away, lost to sight swiftly in twilight dimness.

"What now, effendi?" asked Ali. "Are we to swim this morass?"

"It's full of bottomless quagmires," answered McGrath. "It would be suicide for a man to plunge into it. Not even the piny woods niggers have ever tried to cross it. But there is a way to get to the hill that rises in the middle of it. You can just barely glimpse it, among the branches of the cypresses, see? Years ago, when Ballville and I were boys-and friends-- we discovered an old, old Indian path, a secret, submerged road that led to that hill. There's a cave in the hill, and a woman is imprisoned in that cave. I'm going to it. Do you want to follow me, or to wait for me here? The path is a dangerous one."

"I will go, effendi," answered the Arab.

McGrath nodded in appreciation, and began to scan the trees about him. Presently he found what he was looking for a faint blaze on a huge cypress, an old mark, almost imperceptible. Confidently then, he stepped into the marsh beside the tree. He himself had made that mark, long ago. Scummy water rose over his shoe soles, but no higher. He stood on a flat rock, or rather on a heap of rocks, the topmost of which was just below the stagnant surface. Locating a certain gnarled cypress far out in the shadow of the marsh, he began walking directly toward it, spacing his strides carefully, each carrying him to a rockstep invisible below the murky water. Ali ibn Suleyman followed him, imitating his motions.

Through the swamp they went, following the marked trees that were their guide-posts. McGrath wondered anew at the motives that had impelled the ancient builders of the trail to bring these huge rocks from afar and sink them like piles into the slush. The work must have been stupendous, requiring no mean engineering skill. Why had the Indians built this broken road to Lost Island? Surely that isle and the cave in it had some religious significance to the red men; or perhaps it was their refuge against some stronger foe.

The going was slow; a misstep meant a plunge into marshy ooze, into unstable mire that might swallow a man alive. The island grew out of the trees ahead of them-a small knoll, girdled by a vegetation-choked beach. Through the foliage was visible the rocky wall that rose sheer from the beach to a height of fifty or sixty feet. It was almost like a granite block rising from a flat sandy rim. The pinnacle was almost bare of growth.

McGrath was pale, his breath coming in quick gasps. As they stepped upon the beach-like strip, Ali, with a glance of commiseration, drew a flask from his pocket.

"Drink a little brandy, effendi," he urged, touching the mouth to his own lips, oriental-fashion. "It will aid you."

McGrath knew that Ali thought his evident agitation was a result of exhaustion. But he was scarcely aware of his recent exertions. It was the emotions that raged within him-the thought of Constance Brand, whose beautiful form had haunted his troubled dreams for three dreary years. He gulped deeply of the liquor, scarcely tasting it, and handed back the flask.

"Come on!"

The pounding of his own heart was suffocating, drowning the distant drum, as he thrust through the choking vegetation at the foot of the cliff. On the gray rock above the green mask appeared a curious carven symbol, as he had seen it years ago, when its discovery led him and Richard Ballville to the hidden cavern. He tore aside the clinging vines and fronds, and his breath sucked in at the sight of a heavy iron door set in the narrow mouth that opened in the granite wall.

McGrath's fingers were trembling as they swept over the metal, and behind him he could hear Ali breathing heavily.

Some of the white man's excitement had imparted itself to the Arab. McGrath's hands found the three knobs, forming the apices of a triangle-mere protuberances, not apparent to the sight. Controlling his jumping nerves, he pressed them as Ballville had instructed him, and felt each give slightly at the third pressure. Then, holding his breath, he grasped the bar that was welded in the middle of the door, and pulled. Smoothly, on oiled hinges, the massive portal swung open.

They looked into a wide tunnel that ended in another door, this a grille of steel bars. The tunnel was not dark; it was clean and roomy, and the ceiling had been pierced to allow light to enter, the holes covered with screens to keep out insects and reptiles. But through the grille he glimpsed something that sent him racing along the tunnel, his heart almost bursting through his ribs. Ali was close at his heels.

The grille-door was not locked. It swung outward under his fingers. He stood motionless, almost stunned with the impact of his emotions.

His eyes were dazzled by a gleam of gold; a sunbeam slanted down through the pierced rock roof and struck mellow fire from the glorious profusion of golden hair that flowed over the white arm that pillowed the beautiful head on the carved oak table.

"Constance!" It was a cry of hunger and yearning that burst from his livid lips.

Echoing the cry, the girl started up, staring wildly, her hands at her temples, her lambent hair rippling over her shoulders. To his dizzy gaze she seemed to float in an aureole of golden light.

"Bristol! Bristol McGrath!" she echoed his call with a haunting, incredulous cry. Then she was in his arms, her white arms clutching him in a frantic embrace, as if she feared he were but a phantom that might vanish from her.

For the moment the world ceased to exist for Bristol McGrath. He might have been blind, deaf and dumb to the universe at large. His dazed brain was cognizant only of the woman in his arms, his senses drunken' with the softness and fragrange of her, his soul stunned with the overwhelming realization of a dream he had thought dead and vanished for ever.

When he could think consecutively again, he shook himself like a man coming out of a trance, and stared stupidly around him. He was in a wide chamber, cut in the solid rock. Like the tunnel, it was illumined from above, and the air was fresh and clean. There were chairs, tables and a hammock, carpets on the rocky floor, cans of food and a water-cooler. Ballville had not failed to provide for his captive's comfort. McGrath glanced around at the Arab, and saw him beyond the grille. Considerately he had not intruded upon their reunion.

26

"Three years!" the girl was sobbing. "Three years I've waited. I knew you'd come! I knew it! But we must be careful, my darling. Richard will kill you if he finds youkill us both!"

"He's beyond killing anyone," answered McGrath. "But just the same, we've got to get out of here."

Her eyes flared with new terror.

"Yes! John De Albor! Ballville was afraid of him. That's why he locked me in here. He said he'd sent for you. I was afraid for you-"

"Ali!" McGrath called. "Come in here. We're getting out of here now, and we'd better take some water and food with us. We may have to hide in the swamps for-"

Abruptly Constance shrieked, tore herself from her lover's arms. And McGrath, frozen by the sudden, awful fear in her wide eyes, felt the dull jolting impact of a savage blow at the base of his skull. Consciousness did not leave him, but a strange paralysis gripped him. He dropped like an empty sack on the stone floor and lay there like a dead man, helplessly staring up at the scene which tinged his brain with madness-Constance struggling frenziedly in the grasp of the man he had known as Ali ibn Suleyman, now terribly transformed.

The man had thrown off his turban and glasses. And in the murky whites of his eyes, McGrath read the truth with its grisly implications-the man was not an Arab. He was a negroid mixed breed. Yet some of his blood must have been Arab, for there was a slightly Semitic cast to his countenance, and this cast, together with his oriental garb and his perfect acting of his part, had made him seem genuine. But now all this was discarded and the negroid strain was uppermost; even his voice, which had enunciated the sonorous Arabic, was now the throaty gutturals of the negro.

"You've killed him!" the girl sobbed hysterically, striving vainly to break away from the cruel fingers that prisoned her white wrists.

"He's not dead yet," laughed the octoroon. "The fool quaffed drugged brandy-a drug found only in the Zambebwei jungles. It lies inactive in the system until made effective by a sharp blow on a nerve center."

"Please do something for him!" she begged.

The fellow laughed brutally.

"Why should I? He has served his purpose. Let him lie there until the swamp insects have picked his bones. I should like to watch that-but we will be far away before nightfall." His eyes blazed with the bestial gratification of possession. The sight of this white beauty struggling in his grasp seemed to rouse all the jungle lust in the man. McGrath's wrath and agony found expression only in his bloodshot eyes. He could not move hand or foot.

"It was well I returned alone to the Manor," laughed the octoroon. "I stole up to the window while this fool talked with Richard Ballville. The thought came to me to let him lead me to the place where you were hidden. It had never occurred to me that there was a hiding-place in the swamp. I had the Arab's coat, slippers and turban; I had thought I might use them sometime. The glasses helped, too. It was not difficult to make an Arab out of myself. This man had never seen John De Albor. I was born in East Africa and grew up a slave in the house of an Arabbefore I ran away and wandered to the land of Zambebwei.

"But enough. We must go. The drum has been muttering all day. The blacks are restless. I promised them a sacrifice to Zemba. I was going to use the Arab, but by the time I had tortured out of him the information I desired, he was no longer fit for a sacrifice. Well, let them bang their silly drum. They'd like to have you for the Bride of Zemba, but they don't know I've found you. I have a motor-boat hidden on the river five miles from here-"

"You fool!" shrieked Constance, struggling passionately. "Do you think you can carry a white girl down the river, like a slave?"

"I have a drug which will make you like a dead woman," he said. "You will lie in the bottom of the boat, covered by sacks. When I board the steamer that shall bear us from these shores, you will go into my cabin in a large, well-ventilated trunk. You will know nothing of the discomforts of the voyage. You will awake in Africa--"

He was fumbling in his shirt, necessarily releasing her with one hand. With a frenzied scream and a desperate wrench, she tore loose and sped out through the tunnel. John De Albor plunged after her, bellowing. A red haze floated before McGrath's maddened eyes. The girl would plunge to her death in the swamps, unless she remembered the guide-marks--perhaps it was death she sought, in preference to the fate planned for her by the fiendish negro.

They had vanished from his sight, out of the tunnel; but suddenly Constance screamed again, with a new poignancy. To McGrath's ears came an excited jabbering of negro gutturals. De Albor's accents were lifted in angry protest. Constance was sobbing hysterically. The voices were moving away. McGrath got a vague glimpse of a group of figures through the masking vegetation as they moved across the line of the tunnel mouth. He saw Constance being dragged along by half a dozen giant blacks typical pineland dwellers, and after them came John De Albor, his hands eloquent in dissension. That glimpse only, through the fronds, and then the tunnel mouth gaped empty and the sound of splashing water faded away through 'the marsh.

CHAPTER 4.
THE BLACK GOD'S HUNGER

In the brooding silence of the cavern Bristol McGrath lay staring blankly upward, his soul a seething hell. Fool, fool, to be taken in so easily! Yet, how could he have known? He had never seen De Albor; he had supposed he was a fullblooded negro. Ballville had called him a black beast, but he must have been referring to his soul. De Albor, but for the betraying murk of his eyes, might pass anywhere for a white man.

The presence of those black men meant but one thing: they had followed him and De Albor, had seized Constance as she rushed from the cave. De Albor's evident fear bore a hideous implication; he had said the blacks wanted to sacrifice Constance-now she was in their hands.

"God!" The word burst from McGrath's lips, startling in the stillness, startling to the speaker. He was electrified; a few moments before he had been dumb. But now he discovered he could move his lips, his tongue. Life was stealing back through his dead limbs; they stung as if with returning circulation. Frantically he encouraged that sluggish flow. Laboriously he worked his extremities, his fingers, hands, wrists and finally, with a surge of wild triumph, his arms and legs. Perhaps De Albor's hellish drug had lost some of

31

its power through age. Perhaps McGrath's unusual stamina threw off the effects as another man could not have done.

The tunnel door had not been closed, and McGrath knew why; they did not want to shut out the insects which would soon dispose of a helpless body; already the pests were streaming through the door, a noisome horde.

McGrath rose at last, staggering drunkenly, but with his vitality surging more strongly each second. When he tottered from the cave, no living thing met his glare. Hours had passed since the negroes had departed with their prey. He strained his ears for the drum. It was silent. The stillness rose like an invisible black mist around him. Stumblingly he splashed along the rock-trail that led to hard ground. Had the blacks taken their captive back to the death-haunted Manor, or deeper into the pinelands?

Their tracks were thick in the mud: half a dozen pairs of bare, splay feet, the slender prints of Constance's shoes, the marks of De Albor's Turkish slippers. He followed them with increasing difficulty as the ground grew higher and harder.

He would have missed the spot where they turned off the dim trail but for the fluttering of a bit of silk in the faint breeze. Constance had brushed against a tree-trunk there, and the rough bark had shredded off a fragment of her dress. The band had been headed east, toward the Manor. At the spot where the bit of cloth hung, they had turned sharply southward. The matted pine needles showed no tracks, but disarranged vines and branches bent aside marked their progress, until McGrath, following these signs, came out upon another trail leading southward.

Here and there were marshy spots, and these showed the prints of feet, bare and shod. McGrath hastened along the trail, pistol in hand, in full possession of his faculties at last. His face was grim and pale. De Albor had not had an opportunity to disarm him after striking that treacherous blow. Both the octoroon and the blacks of the pinelands believed him to be lying helpless back in Lost Cave. That, at least, was to his advantage.

He kept straining his ears in vain for the drum he had heard earlier in the day. The silence did not reassure him. In a voodoo sacrifice drums would be thundering, but he knew he was dealing with something even more ancient and abhorrent than voodoo.

Voodoo was comparatively a young religion, after all, born in the hills of Haiti. Behind the froth of voodooism rose the grim religions of Africa, like granite cliffs glimpsed through a mask of green fronds. Voodooism was a mewling infant beside the black, immemorial colossus that had reared its terrible shape in the older land through uncounted ages, Zambebwei! The very name sent a shudder through him, symbolic of horror and fear. It was more than the name of a country and the mysterious tribe that inhabited that country;

it signified something fearfully old and evil, something that had survived its natural epoch-a religion of the Night, and a deity whose name was Death and Horror.

He had seen no negro cabins. He knew these were farther to the east and south, most of them, huddling along the banks of the river and the tributary creeks. It was the instinct of the black man to build his habitation by a river, as he had built by the Congo, the Nile and the Niger since Time's first gray dawn. Zambebwei! The word beat like a throb of a tom-tom through the brain of Bristol McGrath. The soul of the black man had not changed, through the slumberous centuries. Change might come in the clangor of city streets, in the raw rhythms of Harlem; but the swamps of the Mississippi do not differ enough from the swamps of the Congo to work any great transmutation in the spirit of a race that was old before the first white king wove the thatch of his wattled hut-palace.

Following that winding path through the twilight dimness of the big pines, McGrath did not find it in his soul to marvel that black slimy tentacles from the depths of Africa had stretched across the world to breed nightmares in an alien land. Certain natural conditions produce certain effects, breed certain pestilences of body or mind, regardless of their geographical situation. The river-haunted pinelands were as abysmal in their way as were the reeking African jungles.

The trend of the trail was away from the river. The land sloped very gradually upward, and all signs of marsh vanished.

The trail widened, showing signs of frequent use. McGrath became nervous. At any moment he might meet someone. He took to the thick woods alongside the trail, and forced his way onward, each movement sounding cannon-loud to his whetted ears. Sweating with nervous tension, he came presently upon a smaller path, which meandered in the general direction he wished to go. The pinelands were crisscrossed by such paths.

He followed it with greater ease and stealth, and presently, coming to a crook in it, saw it join the main trail. Near the point of junction stood a small log cabin, and between him and the cabin squatted a big black man. This man was hidden behind the bole of a huge pine beside the narrow path, and peering around it toward the cabin. Obviously he was spying on someone, and it was quickly apparent who this was, as John De Albor came to the door and stared despairingly down the wide trail. The black watcher stiffened and lifted his fingers to his mouth as if to sound a far-carrying whistle, but De Albor shrugged his shoulders helplessly and turned back into the cabin again. The negro relaxed, though he did not alter his vigilance.

What this portended, McGrath did not know, nor did he pause to speculate. At the sight of De Albor a red mist turned the sunlight to blood, in which the black body before him floated like an ebony goblin.

A panther stealing upon its kill would have made as much noise as McGrath made in his glide down the path toward the squatting black. He was aware of no personal animosity toward the man, who was but an obstacle in his path of vengeance. Intent on the cabin, the black man did not hear that stealthy approach. Oblivious to all else, he did not move or turn-until the pistol butt descended on his woolly skull with an impact that stretched him senseless among the pine needles.

McGrath crouched above his motionless victim, listening. There was no sound near by-but suddenly, far away, there rose a long-drawn shriek that shuddered and died away. The blood congealed in McGrath's veins. Once before he had heard that sound-in the low forest-covered hills that fringe the borders of forbidden Zambebwei; his black boys had turned the color of ashes and fallen on their faces. What it was he did not know; and the explanation offered by the shuddering natives had been too monstrous to be accepted by a rational mind. They called it the voice of the god of Zambebwei.

Stung to action, McGrath rushed down the path and hurled himself against the back door of the cabin. He did not know how many blacks were inside; he did not care. He was beserk with grief and fury.

The door crashed inward under the impact. He lit on his feet inside, crouching, gun leveled hip-high, lips asnarl.

But only one man faced him--John De Albor, who sprang to his feet with a startled cry. The gun dropped from McGrath's fingers. Neither lead nor steel could glut his hate now. It must be with naked hands, turning back the pages of civilization to the red dawn days of the primordial.

With a growl that was less like the cry of a man than the grunt of a charging lion, McGrath's fierce hands locked about the octoroon's throat. De Albor was borne backward by the hurtling impact, and the men crashed together over a camp cot, smashing it to ruins. And as they tumbled on the dirt floor, McGrath set himself to kill his enemy with his bare fingers.

The octoroon was a tall man, rangy and strong. But against the berserk white man he had no chance. He was hurled about like a sack of straw, battered and smashed savagely against the floor, and the iron fingers that were crushing his throat sank deeper and deeper until his tongue protruded from his gaping blue lips and his eyes were starting from his head. With death no more than a hand's breadth from the octoroon, some measure of sanity returned to McGrath.

He shook his head like a dazed bull; eased his terrible grip a trifle, and snarled: "Where is the girl? Quick, before I kill you!"

De Albor retched and fought for breath, ashen-faced. "The blacks!" he gasped. "They have taken her to be the Bride of Zemba! I could not prevent them. They demand a sacrifice. I offered them you, but they said you were paralyzed and would die anyway-they were cleverer than I thought. They followed me back to the Manor from the spot where we left, the Arab in the road-followed us from the Manor to the island.

"They are out of hand-mad with blood-lust. But even I, who know black men as none else knows them, I had forgotten that not even a priest of Zambebwei can control them when the fire of worship runs in their veins. I am their priest and master-yet when I sought to save the girl, they forced me into this cabin and set a man to watch me until the sacrifice is over. You must have killed him; he would never have let you enter here."

With a chill grimness, McGrath picked up his pistol.

"You came here as Richard Ballville's friend," he said unemotionally. "To get possession of Constance Brand, you made devil-worshippers out of the black people. You deserve death for that. When the European authorities that govern Africa catch a priest of Zambebwei, they hang him. You have admitted that you are a priest. Your life is forfeit on that score, too. But it is because of your hellish teachings that Constance Brand is to die, and it's for that reason that I'm going to blow out your brains."

John De Albor shriveled. "She is not dead yet," he gasped, great drops of perspiration dripping from his ashy face. "She will not die until the moon is high above the pines. It is full tonight, the Moon of Zambebwei. Don't kill me. Only I can save her. I know I failed before. But if I go to them, appear to them suddenly and without warning, they'll think it is because of supernatural powers that I was able to escape from the but without being seen by the watchman. That will renew my prestige.

"You can't save her. You might shoot a few blacks, but there would still be scores left to kill you-and her. But I have a plan-yes, I am a priest of Zambebwei. When I was a boy I ran away from my Arab master and wandered far until I came to the land of Zambebwei. There I grew to manhood and became a priest, dwelling there until the white blood in me drew me out in the world again to learn the ways of the white men. When I came to America I brought a Zemba with me-I can not tell you how.

"Let me save Constance Brand!" He was clawing at McGrath, shaking as if with an ague. "I love her, even as you love her. I will play fair with you both, I swear it! Let me save her! We can fight for her later, and I'll kill you if I can."

The frankness of that statement swayed McGrath more than anything else the octoroon could have said. It was a desperate gamble-but after all, Constance would be no worse off with John De Albor alive than she was already. She would be dead before midnight unless something was done swiftly.

"Where is the place of sacrifice?" asked McGrath.

"Three miles away, in an open glade," answered De Albor. "South on the trail that runs past my cabin. All the blacks are gathered there except my guard and some others who are watching the trail below the cabin. They are scattered out along it, the nearest out of sight of my cabin, but within sound of the loud, shrill whistle with which these people signal one another.

"This is my plan. You wait here in my cabin, or in the woods, as you choose. I'll avoid the watchers on the trail, and appear suddenly before the blacks at the House of Zemba. A sudden appearance will impress them deeply, as I said. I know I can not persuade them to abandon their plan, but I will make them postpone the sacrifice until just before dawn. And before that time I will manage to steal the girl and flee with her. I'll return to your hiding-place, and we'll fight our way out together."

McGrath laughed. "Do you think I'm an utter fool? You'd send your blacks to murder me, while you carried Constance away as you planned. I'm going with you. I'll hide at the edge of the clearing, to help you if you need help. And if you make a false move, I'll get you, if I don't get anybody else."

The octoroon's murky eyes glittered, but he nodded acquiescence.

"Help me bring your guard into the cabin," said McGrath. "He'll be coming to soon. We'll tie and gag him and leave him here."

The sun was setting and twilight was stealing over the pinelands as McGrath and his strange companion stole through the shadowy woods. They had circled to the west to avoid the watchers on the trail, and were now following on the many narrow footpaths which traced their way through the forest. Silence reigned ahead of them, and McGrath mentioned this.

"Zemba is a god of silence," muttered De Albor. "From sunset to sunrise on the night of the full moon, no drum is beaten. If a dog barks, it must be slain; if a baby cries, it must be killed. Silence locks the jaws of the people until Zemba roars. Only his voice is lifted on the night of the Moon of Zemba."

McGrath shuddered. The foul deity was an intangible spirit, of course, embodied only in legend; but De Albor spoke of it as a living thing.

A few stars were blinking out, and shadows crept through the thick woods, blurring the trunks of the trees that melted together in darkness. McGrath knew they could not be far from the House of Zemba. He sensed the close presence of a throng of people, though he heard nothing.

De Albor, ahead of him, halted suddenly, crouching. McGrath stopped, trying to pierce the surrounding mask of interlacing branches.

"What is it?" muttered the white man, reaching for his pistol.

De Albor shook his head, straightening. McGrath could not see the stone in his hand, caught up from the earth as he stooped.

"Do you hear something?" demanded McGrath.

De Albor motioned him to lean forward, as if to whisper in his ear. Caught off his guard, McGrath bent toward him—even so he divined the treacherous African's intention, but it was too late. The stone in De Albor's hand crashed sickeningly against the white man's temple. McGrath went down like a slaughtered ox, and De Albor sped away down the path to vanish like a ghost in the gloom.

CHAPTER 5.
THE VOICE OF ZEMBA

In the darkness of the woodland path McGrath stirred at last, and staggered groggily to his feet. That desperate blow might have crushed the skull of a man whose physique and vitality were not that of a bull. His head throbbed and there was dried blood on his temple; but his strongest sensation was burning scorn at himself for having again fallen victim to John De Albor. And yet, who would have suspected that move? He knew De Albor would kill him if he could, but he had not expected an attack before the rescue of Constance. The fellow was dangerous and unpredictable as a cobra. Had his pleas to be allowed to attempt Constance's rescue been but a ruse to escape death at the hands of McGrath?

McGrath stared dizzily at the stars that gleamed through the ebon branches, and sighed with relief to see that the moon had not yet risen. The pinewoods were black as only pinelands can be, with a darkness that was almost tangible, like a substance that could be cut with a knife.

McGrath had reason to be grateful for his rugged constitution. Twice that day had John De Albor outwitted him, and twice the white man's iron frame had survived the attack. His gun was in his scabbard, his knife in its sheath. De Albor had not paused to search, had not paused for a second stroke to make sure. Perhaps there had been a tinge of panic in the African's actions.

Well,--this did not change matters a great deal. He believed that De Albor would make an effort to save the girl. And McGrath intended to be on hand, whether to play a lone hand, or to aid the octoroon. This was no time to hold grudges, with the girl's life at stake. He groped down the path, spurred by a rising glow in the east.

He came upon the glade almost before he knew it. The moon hung in the low branches, blood-red, high enough to illumine it and the throng of black people who squatted in a vast semicircle about it, facing the moon. Their rolling eyes gleamed milkily in the shadows, their features were grotesque masks. None spoke. No head turned toward the bushes behind which he crouched.

He had vaguely expected blazing fires, a blood-stained altar, drums and the chant of maddened worshippers; that would be voodoo. But this was not voodoo, and there was a vast gulf between the two cults. There were no fires, no altars. But the breath hissed through his locked teeth. In a far land he had sought in vain for the rituals of Zambebwei; now he looked upon them within forty miles of the spot where he was born.

In the center of the glade the ground rose slightly to a flat level. On this stood a heavy iron-bound stake that was indeed but the sharpened trunk of a good-sized pine driven deep into the ground. And there was something living chained to that stake-something which caused McGrath to catch his breath in horrified unbelief.

He was looking upon a god of Zambebwei. Stories had told of such creatures, wild tales drifting down from the borders of the forbidden country, repeated by shivering natives about jungle fires, passed along until they reached the ears of skeptical white traders. McGrath had never really believed the stories, though he had gone searching for the being they described. For they spoke of a beast that was a blasphemy against nature-a beast that sought food strange to its natural species.

The thing chained to the stake was an ape, but such an ape as the world at large never dreamed of, even in nightmares. Its shaggy gray hair was shot with silver that shone in the rising moon; it looked gigantic as it squatted ghoulishly on its haunches. Upright, on its bent, gnarled legs, it would be as tall as a man, and much broader and thicker. But its prehensile fingers were armed with talons like those of a tiger-not the heavy blunt nails of the natural anthropoid, but the cruel simitar-curved claws of the great carnivora. Its face was like that of a gorilla, low browed, flaring-nostriled, chinless; but when it snarled, its wide flat nose wrinkled like that of a great cat, and the cavernous mouth disclosed saber-like fangs, the fangs of a beast of prey. This was Zemba, the creature sacred to the people of the land of Zambebwei-a monstrosity, a violation of an accepted law of nature-a carnivorous ape. Men had laughed at the story, hunters and zoologists and traders.

But now McGrath knew that such creatures dwelt in black Zambebwei and were worshipped, as primitive man is prone to worship an obscenity or perversion of nature. Or a survival of past eons: that was what the flesh-eating apes of Zambebwei were-survivors of a forgotten epoch, remnants of a vanished prehistoric age, when nature was experimenting with matter, and life took many monstrous forms.

The sight of the monstrosity filled McGrath with revulsion; it was abysmal, a reminder of that brutish and horrorshadowed past out of which mankind crawled so painfully, eons ago. This thing was an affront to sanity; it belonged in the dust of oblivion with the dinosaur, the mastodon, and the saber-toothed tiger.

It looked massive beyond the stature of modern beasts-shaped on the plan of another age, when all things were cast in a mightier mold. He wondered if the revolver at his hip would have any effect on it; wondered by what dark and subtle means John De Albor had brought the monster from Zambebwei to the pinelands.

But something was happening in the glade, heralded by the shaking of the brute's chain as it thrust forward its nightmare=head.

46

From the shadows of the trees came a file of black men and women, young, naked except for a mantle of monkeyskins and parrot-feathers thrown over the shoulders of each. More regalia brought by John De Albor, undoubtedly. They formed a semicircle at a safe distance from the chained brute, and sank to their knees, bending their heads to the ground before him. Thrice this motion was repeated. Then, rising, they formed two lines, men and women facing one another, and began to dance; at least it might by courtesy be called a dance. They hardly moved their feet at all, but all other parts of their bodies were in constant motion, twisting, rotating, writhing. The measured, rhythmical movements had no connection at all with the voodoo dances McGrath had witnessed. This dance was disquietingly archaic in its suggestion, though even more depraved and bestial-naked primitive passions framed in a cynical debauchery of motion.

No sound came from the dancers, or from the votaries squatting about the ring of trees. But the ape, apparently infuriated by the continued movements, lifted his head and sent into the night the frightful shriek McGrath had heard once before that day-he had heard it in the hills that border black Zambebwei. The brute plunged to the end of his heavy chain, foaming and gnashing his fangs, and the dancers fled like spume blown before a gust of wind. They scattered in all directions--and then McGrath started up in his covert, barely stifling a cry.

From the deep shadows had come a figure, gleaming tawnily in contrast to the black forms about it. It was John De Albor, naked except for a mantle of bright feathers, and on his head a circlet of gold that might have been forged in Atlantis. In his hand he bore a gold wand that was the scepter of the high priests of Zambebwei.

Behind him came a pitiful figure, at the sight of which the moon-lit forest reeled to McGrath's sight.

Constance had been drugged. Her face was that of a sleep-walker; she seemed not aware of her peril, or the fact that she was naked. She walked like a robot, mechanically responding to the urge of the cord tied about her white neck. The other end of that cord was in John De Albor's hand, and he half led, half dragged her toward the horror that squatted in the center of the glade. De Albor's face was ashy in the moonlight that now flooded the glade with molten silver. Sweat beaded his skin. His eyes gleamed with fear and ruthless determination. And in a staggering instant McGrath knew that the man had failed, that he had been unable to save Constance, and that now, to save his own life from his suspicious followers, he himself was dragging the girl to the gory sacrifice.

No vocal sound came from the votaries, but hissing intake of breath sucked through thick lips, and the rows of black bodies swayed like reeds in the wind. The great ape leaped up, his face a slavering devil's mask; he howled with frightful eagerness, gnashing his great fangs, that yearned to sink into that soft white flesh, and the hot blood beneath. He surged against his chain, and the stout post quivered. McGrath, in the bushes, stood frozen, paralyzed by the imminence of horror. And then John De Albor stepped behind the unresisting girl and gave her a powerful push that sent her reeling forward to pitch headlong on the ground under the monster's talons.

And simultaneously McGrath moved. His move was instinctive rather than conscious. His .44 jumped into his hand and spoke, and the great ape screamed like a man death-stricken and reeled, clapping misshapen hands to its head.

An instant the throng crouched frozen, white eyes bulging, jaws hanging slack. Then before any could move, the ape, blood gushing from his head, wheeled, seized the chain in both hands and snapped it with a wrench that twisted the heavy links apart as if they had been paper.

John De Albor stood directly before the mad brute, paralyzed in his tracks. Zemba raored and leaped, and the african went down under him, disemboweled by the razorlike talons, his head crushed to a crimson pulp by a sweep of the great paw.

Ravening, the monster charged among the votaries, clawing and ripping and smiting, screaming intolerably. Zambebwei spoke, and death was in his bellowing Screaming, howling, fighting, the black people scrambled over one another in their mad flight. Men and women went down under those shearing talons, were dismembered by those gnashing fangs. It was a red drama of the primitive-destruction amuck and ariot, the primordial embodied in fangs and talons, gone mad and plunging in slaughter. Blood and brains deluged the earth, black bodies and limbs and fragments of bodies littered the moonlighted glade in ghastly heaps before the last of the howling wretches found refuge among the trees. The sounds of their blundering, panic-stricken flight drifted back.

McGrath had leaped from his covert almost as soon as he had fired. Unnoticed by the terrified negroes, and himself scarcely cognizant of the slaughter raging around him, he raced across the glade toward the pitiful white figure that lay limply beside the iron-bound stake.

"Constance!" he cried, gathering her to his breast.

Languidly she opened her cloudy eyes. He held her close, heedless of the screams and devastation surging about them. Slowly recognition grew in those lovely eyes.

"Bristol!" she murmured, incoherently. Then she screamed, clung to him, sobbing hysterically. "Bristol! They told me you were dead! The blacks! The horrible blacks!

They're going to kill me! They were going to kill De Albor too, but he promised to sacrifice-"

"Don't, girl, don't!" He subdued her frantic tremblings. "It's all right, now-" Abruptly he looked up into the grinning bloodstained face of nightmare and death. The great ape had ceased to rend his dead victims and was slinking toward the living pair in the center of the glade. Blood oozed from the wound in its sloping skull that had maddened it.

McGrath sprang toward it, shielding the prostrate girl; his pistol spurted flame, pouring a stream of lead into the mighty breast as the beast charged.

On it came, and his confidence waned. Bullet after bullet he sent crashing into its vitals, but it did not halt. Now he dashed the empty gun full into the gargoyle face without effect, and with a lurch and a roll it had him in its grasp. As the giant arms closed crushingly about him, he abandoned all hope, but following his fighting instinct to the last, he drove his dagger hilt-deep in the shaggy belly.

But even as he struck, he felt a shudder run through the gigantic frame. The great arms fell away-and then he was hurled to the ground in the last death throe of the monster, and the thing was swaying, its face a deathmask. Dead on its feet, it crumpled, toppled to the ground, quivered and lay still. Not even a man-eating ape of Zambebwei could survive that close-range volley of mushrooming lead.

51

As the man staggered up, Constance rose and reeled into his arms, crying hysterically.

"It's all right now, Constance," he panted, crushing her to him. "The Zemba's dead; De Albor's dead; Ballville's dead; the negroes have run away. There's nothing to prevent us leaving now. The Moon of Zambebwei was the end for them. But it's the beginning of life for us."

THE END

www.ingramcontent.com/pod-product-compliance
Lightning Source LLC
Chambersburg PA
CBHW030239180626
46810CB00008B/3213